OLIV

and the Snow Day

adapted by Farrah McDoogle
based on the screenplay written by Eryk Casemiro & Kate Boutilier
illustrated by Shane L. Johnson

Ready-to-Read

Simon Spotlight
New York   London   Toronto   Sydney

Based on the TV series *OLIVIA*™ as seen on Nickelodeon™

SIMON SPOTLIGHT
An imprint of Simon & Schuster Children's Publishing Division
1230 Avenue of the Americas, New York, New York 10020
Copyright © 2010 Silver Lining Productions Limited (a Chorion company). All rights reserved.
OLIVIA™ and © 2010 Ian Falconer. All rights reserved.
All rights reserved, including the right of reproduction in whole or in part in any form.
SIMON SPOTLIGHT, READY-TO-READ, and colophon are registered trademarks of Simon & Schuster, Inc.
For information about special discounts for bulk purchases, please contact Simon & Schuster
Special Sales at 1-866-506-1949 or business@simonandschuster.com.
Manufactured in the United States of America 0912 LAK
First Simon Spotlight edition, November 2010
7 8 9 10
Library of Congress Cataloging-in-Publication Data
McDoogle, Farrah.
Olivia and the snow day / adapted by Farrah McDoogle ; based on the screenplay written by
Eryk Casemiro & Kate Boutilier. — 1st ed.
p. cm. — (Ready-to-read)
"Based on the TV series, Olivia as seen on Nickelodeon"—Copyright page.
I. Casemiro, Eryk. II. Boutilier, Kate. III. Olivia (Television program) IV. Title.
PZ7.M478445701i 2010
[E]—dc22
2009047167
ISBN 978-1-4423-3638-4 (hc)
ISBN 978-1-4424-0813-5 (pbk)

"Look at all that snow,"
Olivia says to Ian.

"Will school be closed?"
asks Ian.

"Listen to the radio
to find out," says Mother.
Olivia and Ian turn up
the radio.
"Hampshire School is closed

today," says the man
on the radio.
"Yippee!" shout Olivia
and Ian.
Today is a Snow Day!

"I will build a snow fort,"
says Ian.
He gets his hat, boots,
and mittens.

"I have an even better idea,"
says Olivia.

She gets her video camera.

"My viewers need facts
about the Snow Day!"

"I am live at the scene!"
says Reporter Olivia.
"Look at all this snow!
A snowbank is taller
than me!"

Olivia wants to interview someone about the snow. "It is called a Man-on-the-Street interview," Olivia explains to Julian.

Julian does not see a man
or the street.

He only sees snow.

But Olivia sees someone.

"Hello, Man in the Driveway,"
calls Olivia to her father.
"Do you have any thoughts
about the snow?"

"The snow is heavy,"
says Father.
"Exciting!" says Olivia.

Father thinks of an exciting story. "Have you seen the Abominable Snowman?" he asks.

"Who is the Abominable
Snowman?" asks Olivia.
"The Abominable Snowman
is a huge, hairy creature.
It makes huge footprints
in the snow."

Julian looks a little worried.

"Do not worry," says Father.

"Nobody has seen the

Abominable Snowman."

Olivia wants to look for the
Abominable Snowman.
"I owe it to my viewers,"
she explains.
Olivia and Julian borrow
Ian's sled.

Ian loans them his sled,
but he does not join
the search.
Ian prefers to work on his
snow fort.

"Something moved
in the bush!" yells Olivia.
But it is just Perry.

Perry sees something!

"Follow Perry!" Olivia says.

They see huge footprints!

"Roll the video camera," whispers Olivia. Julian films with the video camera.

"Did you hear that?" Olivia asks.

"The Abominable Snowman said my name!"

The huge footprints lead
to a tall snowbank.
Could it be the Abominable
Snowman at last?

No! It is our friend Harold!
He fell into the snowbank.
His snowshoes made
the footprints.

Harold is sorry he is
not as exciting as the
Abominable Snowman.
But Reporter Olivia is
not sorry.
"Roll the video camera!"

"This is Reporter Olivia
live at the scene.
The Abominable Snowman
was captured in my
backyard!
What a great Snow Day!"